A Note to Parents and Caregivers:

Read-it! Readers are for children who are just starting on the amazing road to reading. These beautiful books support both the acquisition of reading skills and the love of books.

The PURPLE LEVEL presents basic topics and objects using high frequency words and simple language patterns.

The RED LEVEL presents familiar topics using common words and repeating sentence patterns.

The BLUE LEVEL presents new ideas using a larger vocabulary and varied sentence structure.

The YELLOW LEVEL presents more challenging ideas, a broad vocabulary, and wide variety in sentence structure.

The GREEN LEVEL presents more complex ideas, an extended vocabulary range, and expanded language structures.

The ORANGE LEVEL presents a wide range of ideas and concepts using challenging vocabulary and complex language structures.

When sharing a book with your child, read in short stretches, pausing often to talk about the pictures. Have your child turn the pages and point to the pictures and familiar words. And be sure to reread favorite stories or parts of stories.

There is no right or wrong way to share books with children. Find time to read with your child, and pass on the legacy of literacy.

Adria F. Klein, Ph.D.
Professor Emeritus
California State University
San Bernardino, California

Editor: Patricia Stockland
Storyboarder: Amy Bailey Muehlenhardt
Page production: JoAnne Nelson/Tracy Davies
Art Director: Keith Griffin
Managing Editor: Catherine Neitge
The illustrations in this book were done in acrylic.

Picture Window Books
5115 Excelsior Boulevard
Suite 232
Minneapolis, MN 55416
877-845-8392
www.picturewindowbooks.com

Printed in the United States of America.

Library of Congress Cataloging-in-Publication Data
Blair, Eric.
Paul Bunyan / by Eric Blair ; illustrated by Micah Chambers-Goldberg.
p. cm. — (Read-it! readers: tall tales)
Summary: Relates some of the legends of Paul Bunyan, a lumberjack said to be taller than
the trees, who had a pet ox named Babe that he once hitched to a road that took too long
to travel and had her pull it straight.
ISBN 1-4048-0976-7 (hardcover)
1. Bunyan, Paul (Legendary character)—Legends. [1. Bunyan, Paul (Legendary
character)—Legends. 2. Folklore—United States. 3. Tall tales.] I. Chambers-Goldberg,
Micah, ill. II. Title. III. Read-it! readers tall tales.
PZ8.1.B5824Pau 2004
398.2'0973'02—dc22   2004018438

Paul Bunyan

By Eric Blair
Illustrated by Micah Chambers-Goldberg

Special thanks to our advisers for their expertise:

Adria F. Klein, Ph.D.
Professor Emeritus, California State University
San Bernardino, California

Susan Kesselring, M.A.
Literacy Educator
Rosemount-Apple Valley-Eagan (Minnesota) School District

PICTURE WINDOW BOOKS
Minneapolis, Minnesota

Paul Bunyan was a big boy.
When he was born,
it took six
giant storks to
deliver him.

His first baby carriage was a
lumber wagon pulled
by oxen.

He ate forty bowls of oatmeal
for breakfast.

Soon, Paul grew so large that his mom had to sew his pants from blankets. His shirts were made from tents.

Before long, Paul grew taller than the trees. He was stronger than any man alive.

Paul was too big to sleep in the house. Instead, he slept in the barn.

Paul and his parents lived in the
Great North Woods.

Sometimes, the weather was so cold that the snow and ice turned blue.

One day, Paul saw a pair of blue eyes in a large snowdrift. When Paul dug into the snow, he found a blue baby ox. The ox was frozen solid.

Paul blew on the baby ox. His giant breath brought the ox back to life.

Babe the Blue Ox became Paul's best friend. Babe grew to be as big as Paul.

Since Paul lived in the Great North
Woods, he decided to become
a lumberjack.

19

Paul became the best lumberjack in the world. He could cut down ten trees with just one swing of his huge ax.

Paul and Babe joined a logging team. They taught the loggers to make giant pancakes. They used shovels to turn the pancakes.

But Paul and Babe missed traveling.

After a while, Paul and Babe left the loggers. The two friends started a new trip to the West.

When it rained, the tracks made by Paul's and Babe's feet filled with water. The tracks became the Great Lakes.

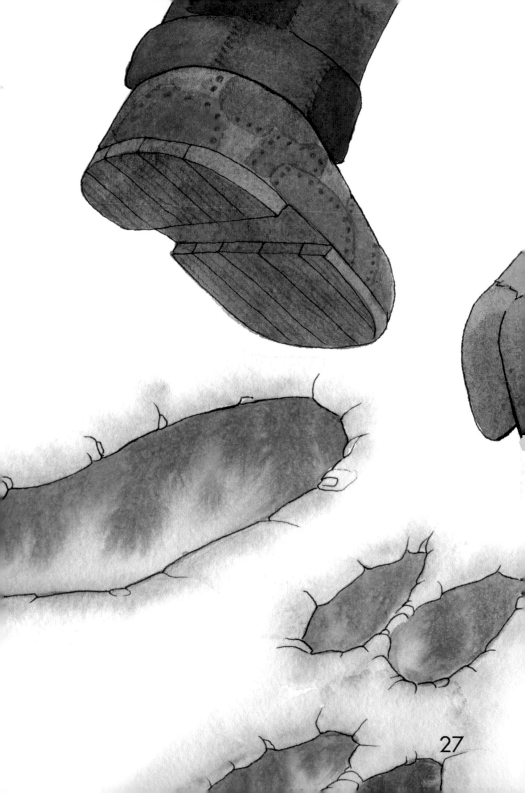

Along the way, Paul and Babe cleared so much forest that the West became treeless.

People called this land the
Great Plains.

Paul and Babe missed all the trees. They decided to return to the Great North Woods.

And that's where they still live today.

More *Read-it!* Readers

Bright pictures and fun stories help you practice your reading skills. Look for more books at your level.

TALL TALES

Annie Oakley, Sharp Shooter by Eric Blair

John Henry by Christianne C. Jones

Johnny Appleseed by Eric Blair

The Legend of Daniel Boone by Eric Blair

Paul Bunyan by Eric Blair

Pecos Bill by Eric Blair

Looking for a specific title or level? A complete list of *Read-it!* Readers is available on our Web site: *www.picturewindowbooks.com*